Young Princesses

AROUND THE WORLD

Isabel Saves the Prince

Based on a True Story of Isabel I of Spain

BY JOAN HOLUB • ILLUSTRATED BY NONNA ALESHINA

ALADDIN PAPERBACKS
An imprint of Simon & Schuster Children's Publishing Division
1230 Avenue of the Americas, New York, NY 10020
Text copyright © 2007 by Joan Holub
Illustrations copyright © 2007 by PiArt & Design Agency
Also available in an Aladdin library edition.
Designed by Karin Paprocki
The text of this book was set in Century Oldstyle BT.
Manufactured in the United States of America
First Aladdin Paperbacks edition August 2007
2 4 6 8 10 9 7 5 3 1
Library of Congress Cataloging-in-Publication Data
Holub, Joan.
Isabel saves the prince : based on a true story of Isabel I of Spain / by Joan Holub ;
illustrated by Nonna Aleshina.—1st Aladdin Paperbacks ed.
p. cm.—(Young princesses around the world) (Ready-to-read. Level 3)
ISBN-13: 978-0-689-87197-9 (pbk.) ISBN-10: 0-689-87197-X (pbk.)
ISBN-13: 978-0-689-87198-6 (lib. bdg.) ISBN-10: 0-689-87198-8 (lib. bdg.)
1. Isabella I, Queen of Spain, 1451–1504—Juvenile literature.
2. Spain—History—Ferdinand and Isabella, 1479–1516—Juvenile literature.
3. Queens—Spain—Biography—Juvenile literature. I. Aleshina, Nonna.
II. Title. III. Series.
DP163.H84 2007
946'.03092—dc22
[B]
2007005514

*For Mary Kay and Monroe
at Pat's Place Bookstore in
Rockport, Texas.
—J. H.*

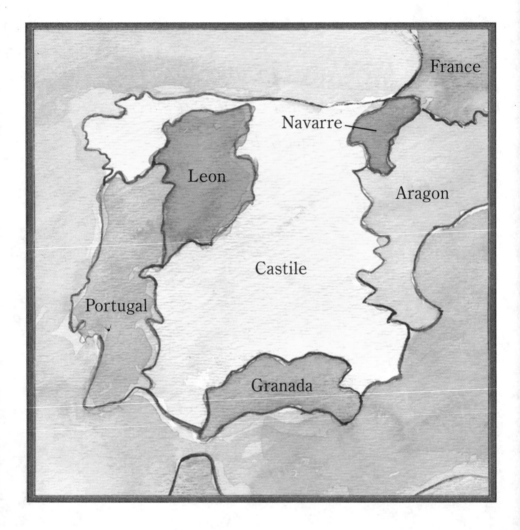

There are Spanish words in this book. Here is what they mean and how to say them:

abuela (ahb-WAY-lah)—**grandmother**

hermano (air-MAH-no)—**brother**

madre (MAH-dray)—**mother**

padre (PAH-dray)—**father**

Most Spanish nouns that end in "-o" name something male. Most Spanish nouns that end in "-a" name something female. Since the Spanish word for **brother** is **hermano**, what do you think the Spanish word for **sister** might be? It's **hermana**!

CHAPTER

1

Isabel Leaves Home

The door to the castle opened with a crash. Three men stomped in.

Ten-year-old Princess Isabel and her younger **hermano** Prince Alfonso watched from upstairs.

"Who are they?" Alfonso whispered.

"Soldiers!" Isabel said in surprise. Soldiers had never come to her home before.

Isabel and Alfonso's **abuela**
rushed downstairs into the castle hall.

"Why are you here?" she asked the
soldiers.

"The king sent us," one of them
answered. He pulled a letter from his
leather pouch and gave it to her.

"That letter is stamped with King
Henry's wax seal," Isabel told Alfonso.
King Henry was their half brother. He ruled
Castile, the kingdom where they lived.

"I wonder what it says," said Alfonso.

Their **abuela** read the letter and frowned.

"The king wants Isabel and Alfonso to go live with him in Madrid?" she said. "No! Please don't take them."

But the soldier had his orders. "The princess and prince must be ready to go in one hour."

9

Abuela walked up the stairs. Her skirt swished and her prayer beads clicked together.

"Follow me," she told Isabel and Alfonso. She took them to their rooms.

The servants began packing the children's things into large wooden trunks.

"Are we really going to the king's castle?" asked Alfonso. He sounded happy.

"I don't want to go!" said Isabel.

"Shush," said Abuela. "The king's word is law. We dare not disobey him."

"May we tell **Madre** good-bye?" Isabel asked.

Abuela shook her head. "No. It would only upset her."

Isabel and Alfonso's **padre** and **madre** had once been king and queen of Castile. When their **padre** died years ago, Henry became the king in his place.

Now their **madre** hid in her room in the castle tower. She was too sad to come out.

"May I at least say good-bye to Beatriz?" Isabel asked. Beatriz was her best friend.

"I'm sorry. There is no time," said **Abuela**.

Isabel quickly wrote a letter to Beatriz instead. King Henry's castle was far away. It might be a long time before she saw her friend again.

An hour later the servants put the children's trunks in the soldiers' wagons.

Abuela hugged Alfonso good-bye.

Then she hugged Isabel.

"Remember to say your prayers," she told her. "And do your best to protect Alfonso."

"Protect him from what?" asked Isabel.

"From people with evil ways," said **Abuela**. "Even though the king belongs to the Catholic Church like we do, I do not trust him. It's up to you to keep Alfonso safe." Isabel wanted to ask more questions. But the soldiers said it was time to go.

As she and her **hermano** rode away with the soldiers, Isabel looked back at the tower window. She waved, just in case her **madre** was watching.

"Farewell, **Madre**," she said in a quiet voice. "I shall miss you."

CHAPTER 2

Isabel in King Henry's Court

It was night when they reached King Henry's castle. As they rode through the gates, Isabel heard music and laughter.

"Is the king having a party?" she wondered aloud.

"You will soon see," said one of the soldiers. "Come inside. The servants will take your trunks to your new bedrooms."

They left their horses and wagons and went up the steps to the castle door.

The soldiers took the children to the castle's feast room. It was noisy and crowded with people. King Henry and his wife, Queen Juana, sat at the biggest table.

The king wore muddy boots and a dirty shirt. His hair and beard were shaggy. The queen wore a fancy dress decorated with jewels and feathers.

Isabel thought King Henry looked like a dirty lion and the queen looked like a peacock.

The king frowned at Isabel and Alfonso. He did not look glad to see them.

Then why did he bring us here? Isabel wondered.

Queen Juana pulled Alfonso to sit on her lap. "What a handsome boy you have become!"

Alfonso laughed.

All around them people were shouting, drinking wine, and dancing wildly. When a pretty woman ran by, King Henry chased after her.

This must be what **Abuela** had meant by people with evil ways, thought Isabel. Life at home had been quiet and full of prayer. What if Alfonso decided Henry's royal court was more fun? How would she protect him from learning bad manners?

Suddenly a man bumped into Isabel and fell in her lap. Wine splashed on her dress.

"Go away!" she shouted, pushing at him.

Queen Juana giggled. "Stop acting like that sour-faced **abuela** of yours. Enjoy yourself."

"But your friends are too wild," said Isabel. "I don't think our **abuela** would want us to be here at your party."

The queen frowned. "Do you think you are too good for us?"

Isabel did not want to make the queen mad.

"No," she said. "I am just tired. Alfonso and I must find our rooms now. It is past time for our evening prayers."

Isabel took Alfonso's hand to lead him away.

"Go ahead and say your prayers," the queen said. "But do not think they can save you from King Henry's plans for you."

"What plans?" Isabel asked in surprise.

The queen smiled in a mean way. "Wedding plans."

"But I'm only ten years old. I can't get married," said Isabel.

"King Henry will promise you to the richest man who offers," said the queen. "You will marry him when you turn fifteen."

"What if the man is old or ugly?" asked Alfonso.

"Or stupid?" asked Isabel.

"It will not matter," said the queen.

"I understand," said Isabel. She wanted to cry. But she tried to be brave.

3

Isabel Goes to the Fair

Isabel and Alfonso lived in Henry's castle for many weeks.

One day they went to a great trade fair in the town of Medina del Campo. Dozens of merchants had come there to sell goods. King Henry sent soldiers to watch over the two children as they shopped.

"Isabel!" a voice called suddenly. It was Beatriz, Isabel's best friend from home!

27

The two girls hugged.

"I have missed you since you moved away. What is it like living with Horrible Henry?" asked Beatriz.

"Careful," Isabel whispered. "Don't let the king's soldiers hear you."

She pulled Beatriz into a shop. The soldiers waited for them outside, looking bored.

"They cannot hear us now," said Beatriz. "So tell me about King Henry."

"The king is foolish," said Isabel. "He tells jokes about the Catholic saints. And I don't even think he says prayers!"

Beatriz gasped. She was shocked that a Catholic king did not say prayers.

When the girls stepped outside again, Alfonso waved to them from a bookshop.

"Come look at this!" he called.

They went to the shop. He showed them a book called *The Travels of Marco Polo*.

"I have heard of Marco Polo," said Isabel. "He was the famous explorer who went to China many years ago."

"If I went to China, I would bring back barrels of cinnamon," said Alfonso.

"I would bring back beautiful silks to

make dresses," Beatriz said dreamily.

"Spices and silks may soon be easier to get," the shopkeeper said. "Explorers are searching for shorter sea routes to Asia."

"Maybe someday a ship will sail west from our kingdom and find the fastest route of all!" said Alfonso.

Beatriz laughed. "Impossible!"

"But just imagine if it were possible!" said Isabel. "You and Alfonso would get silks and cinnamon much quicker!"

As they all left the shop, Isabel yawned. "I am tired. Queen Juana's parties are so loud that it is hard to sleep at night."

"I like parties," said Alfonso. He grinned and ran ahead.

"King Henry's castle is no place for you and Alfonso. Why do you have to live there?" asked Beatriz.

"I think the king wants to spy on us. He is afraid we might be plotting against him," said Isabel.

"You mean he thinks you want to overthrow him?" asked Beatriz.

"Yes," said Isabel. "There is talk that a group of noblemen is planning to take over his kingdom. They want to crown Alfonso as king in his place."

Suddenly Beatriz pointed at something farther down the lane. "Are those the noblemen with Alfonso now?" she asked.

Isabel turned to see two men speaking to her **hermano**. They looked rich and sneaky.

"Oh no! They probably *are* noblemen. If the soldiers see Alfonso talking to them, they will tell King Henry. He will think Alfonso is plotting against him. Alfonso might go to prison," said Isabel.

"What should we do?" asked Beatriz.

"I will get the soldiers' attention," said Isabel. "You get Alfonso."

Beatriz nodded and hurried off.

Quickly Isabel threw her purse under a bush. Then she walked away.

"Help! My coin purse is gone!" she shouted.

King Henry's soldiers rushed to her side. "Did a thief steal it?" asked one of them.

Isabel wanted to help Alfonso, but she would not tell a lie.

"I did not see any thief, but my coin purse is gone!" she said.

"We will help you find it," said one of the soldiers. They began to search.

A few minutes later Isabel pointed to the ground by the bush.

"Oh! There is my purse after all," she said. "I must have dropped it."

37

Meanwhile, Beatriz pulled Alfonso away from the noblemen. She brought him toward Isabel.

The noblemen slipped away before they could be caught. But the king's soldiers had already seen them talking with Alfonso.

"Who were those men? What were they saying?" a soldier asked him.

Alfonso looked afraid.

Isabel put her arm around him.

"Leave him alone," she told the soldier.

The soldier looked angry. "We will go see King Henry. He will have questions for the prince when he hears of this."

They took Isabel and Alfonso back to their horses. Isabel barely had time to wave to Beatriz before they rode away.

CHAPTER

4

Isabel Protects Alfonso

Soon they were on their way back to the castle.

"Those noblemen at the fair said they want to overthrow King Henry," Alfonso whispered to Isabel. "They think I should be the king instead of him."

"That is treason!" said Isabel. "Do not listen to them. The king will punish you if you do."

Alfonso nodded, but he seemed unsure.

The king frowned at Isabel and Alfonso when they stood before him at the castle.

"Who were the men talking to you at the fair?" he asked Alfonso.

Alfonso was too scared to speak.

Isabel thought quickly. Maybe the truth would protect her **hermano**.

"They were noblemen trying to plot against you," she told the king. "Alfonso did not know them. But he could not get away from them until Beatriz helped. He is just a small boy, after all."

The king was angry. He didn't trust them. But he could not prove they had done anything wrong.

"All right. You may both go. But I will be watching you closely from now on," he warned.

Isabel curtseyed. She had saved Alfonso. **Abuela** would be proud of her.

That night Queen Juana came into the royal chapel during Isabel's prayers.

"My **hermano** is coming tomorrow," she told Isabel. "If he likes you, he may offer to marry you."

"But he is twice my age!" said Isabel.

"He is very rich," snapped the queen. "You will marry him if the king orders you to do so."

Isabel bowed her head.

When the queen left, Isabel finished
her prayers. She prayed for Alfonso's
safety. And she prayed King Henry
would not force her to marry the queen's
hermano.

"I will always try to be a good person,"
she promised herself. "And I pray that
I will always do what is best for my
kingdom."

CHAPTER

5

Queen Isabel

Isabel never did marry a man the king chose. At eighteen she chose her own husband—handsome Prince Ferdinand of Aragon. Their marriage joined Spain's two largest kingdoms, Castile and Aragon.

Isabel and Ferdinand were in love. They thought alike. Both wanted everyone in Spain to be Catholic. They punished anyone who was not.

In 1492 Isabel helped pay for Christopher Columbus's trip across the Atlantic Ocean in search of Asia. During Queen Isabel and King Ferdinand's rule, Spain became the most powerful nation in the world.

This time line lists important events in Isabel's life:

1451	Princess Isabel is born on April 22. She is the daughter of Queen Isabel and King Juan II, rulers of Castile, Spain.
1453	Her brother Prince Alfonso is born.
1454	Her father dies. Her half brother Henry becomes king.
1461	Isabel and Alfonso move to King Henry's court.
1465	Rebel noblemen crown Alfonso king of Castile. This starts a war with King Henry.
1466	Henry tries to make fifteen-year-old Isabel marry a man she dislikes. The man dies before the wedding.
1468	Alfonso dies, probably from plague.
1469	Isabel secretly marries Prince Ferdinand of Aragon, Spain.
1470	The first of Isabel's five children is born.
1474	Henry dies. Isabel is crowned queen of Castile.
1480	A group called the Spanish Inquisition tries to force everyone in Spain to become Christian.
1486	Christopher Columbus asks Isabel to pay for his trip across the Atlantic Ocean. He hopes to find a new route to Asia by sailing west from Spain.
1492	Isabel finally agrees to help Columbus. He sails on August 3 and lands in the Bahama Islands on October 12.
1493	Columbus returns to Spain mistakenly believing he has found Asia.
1504	Queen Isabel dies on November 26 at age 53.